RETURN TO THE
LIBRARY OF DOOM

INKFOOT

BY MICHAEL DAHL

Illu

www.raintreepublishers.co.uk
Visit our website to find out
more information about
Raintree books.

To order:
 Phone 0845 6044371
Fax +44 (0) 1865 312263
Email myorders@raintreepublishers.co.uk

Customers from outside the UK please telephone +44 1865 312262

Raintree is an imprint of Capstone Global Library Limited, a company
incorporated in England and Wales having its registered office at 7 Pilgrim
Street, London, EC4V 6LB – Registered company number: 6695582

Text © Stone Arch Books 2011
First published in the United Kingdom in hardback and paperback by
Capstone Global Library Ltd in 2011
The moral rights of the proprietor have been asserted.

Art Director: Kay Fraser
Graphic Designer: Hilary Wacholz
Production Specialist: Michelle Biedscheid
Originated by Capstone Global Library Ltd
Printed in and bound in China by Leo Paper Products Ltd

ISBN 978 1 406 22506 8 (hardback)
15 14 13 12 11
10 9 8 7 6 5 4 3 2 1

ISBN 978 1 406 22513 6 (paperback)
15 14 13 12 11
10 9 8 7 6 5 4 3 2 1

British Library Cataloguing in Publication Data
A full catalogue record for this book is available from the British Library.

Contents

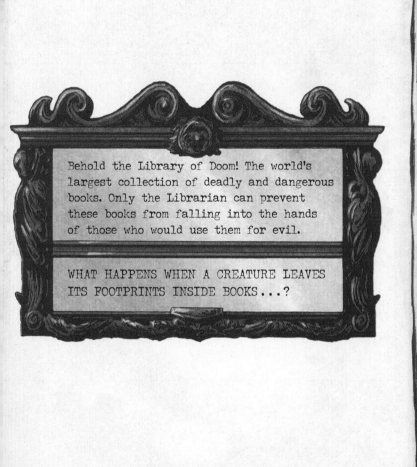

Behold the Library of Doom! The world's largest collection of deadly and dangerous books. Only the Librarian can prevent these books from falling into the hands of those who would use them for evil.

WHAT HAPPENS WHEN A CREATURE LEAVES ITS FOOTPRINTS INSIDE BOOKS...?

Chapter 1

WET

"What's wrong with Bronco?" asks Owen's mother.

BRONCO is Owen's dog.

He has owned Bronco since the dog was a puppy.

Owen hears Bronco **growling** and barking outside.

"You'd better go and bring him inside," says Owen's mother.

"Maybe he's got a **BEAR!**" says Owen's little brother, Doug.

Owen takes his torch and steps
outside.

Bronco has **STOPPED** barking.

"Where are you, boy?" calls Owen.

Owen's family lives in a town in the **MOUNTAINS**.

No one has ever seen a bear in the town before.

But Owen knows there is **ALWAYS** a first time.

Something big and dark crashes through the bushes by the garden shed.

Owen sees another dark shape LYING inside the garden shed.

"Bronco!" yells Owen.

The dog is quiet. He is still breathing, but his eyes are **SHUT**.

On the ground near Bronco's body are large **FOOTPRINTS**.

They are not bear prints. They are bigger than bear prints.

Owen also sees a book. It is an **overdue** library book.

He must have left it in the shed.

Owen knows he will have to **PAY** a huge fine.

Owen reaches out his hand to pet his injured dog.

The fur is wet. *Blood?* wonders Owen.

Owen **SHINES** his torch on his wet hand.

It is covered in thick, black liquid.

Chapter 2

STRANGE SCRATCHES

Owen's mother called the vet after

Owen carried Bronco inside.

Owen and the vet both *LEAN* over the dog.

The vet wears gloves. He carefully checks Bronco's body.

"He's been scratched," says the vet. "It looks **BAD**."

Then the vet looks closely at Bronco's eyes.

"I think your dog has been poisoned," he says.

"Poisoned?" exclaims Owen's little brother.

"I've never seen SCRATCHES
like these before," says the vet.
"I'm not sure what kind of animal
attacked Bronco."

Then the vet looks at Owen's
mother. "I think I should take the
DOG back with me," he says.

The vet **drives** off with Bronco
in his back seat.

"Don't worry," says Owen's mother. "The vet will know what to do."

But how could he? wonders Owen. He said he'd **never** seen scratches like that before.

Who – or what – made those **footprints?**

Chapter 3

BACK TO THE LIBRARY

Owen grabs his torch and goes back outside.

He **RETURNS** to the shed and picks up the library book. "This book is months overdue," he says to himself.

Owen doesn't have the money to pay the fine.

Then he **REMEMBERS** another book.

It was a book in the library that he loved to look through.

It had **PHOTOS** of every kind of animal's footprints.

Owen would be able to find the footprints of the animal that **HURT** his dog.

Then the vet would know how to treat Bronco. The boy glances quickly at his house.

Then he stuffs the book into his coat pocket, and starts **running** down the road.

The woods are dark and cold.

Snowflakes fall from the frozen sky.

A few times, Owen hears growls

from behind the trees.

Each time he does, the library book

seems to SQUIRM in his pocket.

Chapter 4

FOOTPRINTS AND FOOTNOTES

Finally, Owen sees the light up ahead. He darts through the library door.

No one else is inside the library except for Ms Eel.

"Almost **CLOSING** time, Owen,"
says Ms Eel. "I'm getting ready to go
home."

"I'll be quick," says Owen.

He sets the overdue book on the
counter.

Then he **RUNS** towards a corner
of the library.

It is the reference section.

His eyes scan the titles of books on animals and **HUNTING**.

"There's the book," whispers Owen.

He **PULLS** a thick book from the top shelf.

The book is **FULL** of hundreds of photos.

Each photo shows an animal's footprints.

But something is **WRONG** with the book.

rrooowwwggggg

Rrrrwwwooogggllllll   4 Hrroogh

Yaaauuuuugggghhhh   7 Adaawwwrrgghhh

Yyeeeaaauuuwawaaa   10 Sssccrneeeceee

13 Uuooogghhhlaaa   14 Sshhrraaaackaka www 18

16 Jrawwwillooo   17 Aaawwrrggghhh   20 Hrrrrrrogh

19 Grrooowwwwggggg   23 RRrrrwwwooogglll

22 OooAaaauugghhh

26 Yaaauuuugggghhhh   27 Grrrooowww

28 Woouuorrgghhh   29 Yyeeeaaauuuwar   31 RRrroorrg

RRrrrwwwooogglllll   33 RRrrrwwwoog

Sssccrrneeeeceee   33 RRrrrwwwwaac

35 Uuooogghhhlaaa   36 Sshhraaaac

38 Hrrrrrrooughhh   39 Jrawwwww   42 Hrrr

41 Sshhrraaaackakawww   45 Grobooohhhhhl

44 Hrroogh   45 Yyeeeaaa   49 Yyeeeaaa

48 Waauuugghhh

51 Grooooohhhlll   52 Hrrrrr

The 55 Waauuugghhh   56 Yaaauu

58 Oonauugah   59 Ssscertte

61 Yaaauuuugggghhhh   62

oooooowwwwww

On page after page, the **PHOTOS**
are covered up.

Some are crowded off the page.

The book has been filled with
strange **FOOTNOTES**.

41 wwwwwwahhhh

56 gggggrrrrrrrwwwwww

Owen **FLICKS** through more
and more pages.

He can't find the footprints he is
looking for.

Ms Eel walks down the aisle.

"Owen," she says, "did you know there's a **BIG** fine on that book you brought back?"

Then she looks over the boy's shoulder and sees the reference book.

Ms Eel gasps. "Not again!" she whispers.

Chapter 5

THE LEGEND

Owen watches Ms Eel's eyes
GROW wide with fear.

Ms Eel suddenly pulls another book off the shelf and **OPENS** it.

Then she grabs another and another. She opens each book and **THROWS** it to the floor.

Then Ms Eel glances around the empty library. "We have to get out of here," she says.

"What's going on?" asks Owen.

"It's here again," says Ms Eel. "We have to leave. NOW!"

"What's here?" asks Owen. He hears a loud growl outside the library door.

Ms Eel **freezes**.

Then she grabs Owen's hand. "Get in the back room," she says. "Hurry!"

The growl **GROWS** louder.

Suddenly, several books fly off the shelves.

Ms Eel **SCREAMS** and covers her head.

Owen and Ms Eel run into the back room of the library. She quickly **TURNS** and locks the door behind them.

The woman stares **nervously** through a small window in the door.

"What's going on?" demands Owen. "And what's wrong with all the books?"

Ms Eel kneels down. "Have you ever heard of **INKFOOT?**" she asks quietly.

Owen frowns. "You mean Bigfoot?" he asks.

"No, Inkfoot," says Ms Eel. "Bigfoot is just a myth. Inkfoot is real."

"He **HIDES** inside books," explains Ms Eel. "Most people never know he even exists, until he comes out of the books. And he never does that unless something makes him **ANGRY**. Or frightens him."

Like a barking dog? Owen thinks to himself.

Ms Eel grabs the book that Owen was still holding.

"See these pages?" she says. "Footnotes. That's how you **FOLLOW** his trail."

Owen stares down at the pages.

He looks at the footnotes covering

the photos.

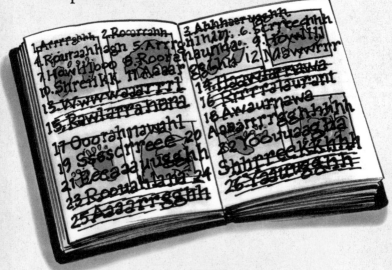

He thinks of the **INK** that

covered Bronco's fur.

Owen needs to tell the vet about Inkfoot.

"We have to call for **HELP**," he says.

"There's no phone back here," says Ms. Eel. "I don't have a mobile with me. Do you?"

Owen shakes his head.

Owen stands up and looks out through the door's **WINDOW**.

Facing the window is a tall bookcase filled with books.

In the spines of the books, Owen sees a **dark** shape.

The shadow stretches from the
bottom shelf all the way to the top.

The shadow seems to cover at least a
hundred books.

It looks like a gigantic, **hairy** beast.

Chapter 6

INKFOOT

"It's out there," says Owen.

The creature's growls fill the library.

Shadowy arms throw books and shelves to the floor.

They **hurl** chairs against tables.

Hairy fists **smash** through computer screens.

"I can't see it now," says the boy.

Then he looks down at the floor of the library's main room.

A **DARK** puddle covers the carpet.

The puddle is GROWING.

"Owen!" yells Ms Eel. "Look!"

Ink is **seeping** through the bottom of the door.

Soon, the ink is several feet deep. The thick, dark liquid **SWIRLS** through the room.

"Don't touch it," says Owen. "It's poison!"

Owen looks at Ms Eel. She is touching a shiny brooch pinned to her sweater.

It is shaped like the letter L. The L begins to **GLOW**.

A **WHIRLPOOL** forms in the middle of the room.

The ink begins to drain away, pouring down the sides of a huge well.

Suddenly, a man FLIES up from the well.

He wears a long, **dark** coat and dark glasses.

"The Librarian!" shouts Ms Eel.

"I came as soon as I saw your signal," says the man, nodding at her **BROOCH**.

He flies out the door of the back room and into the library.

The shadow of Inkfoot rises up among the bookshelves.

The Librarian raises his hands. A powerful wind blows from his fingertips.

The monster's shadow **BREAKS** into small, square pieces.

"Here is Inkfoot," says the man.
"Or, at least what's left of him."

The Librarian shows a piece
of paper to Ms Eel. It is a sheet of
ENDNOTES.

Then the wind blows Owen's
overdue book into the Librarian's
hands.

The **man** looks down at it and grins.

"If you don't mind, Ms Eel," says the Librarian. "Now this book has been returned, I think we should **RETURN** the library to normal."

The man **claps** the covers of the book together.

A blaze of lightning **FLASHES** through the library.

Owen and Ms Eel both gasp. The library has been **returned** to normal.

All the books are back in their place. The computers and chairs are no longer **smashed**.

Ms Eel looks up at the clock. "Closing time," she says.

She tells Owen <u>NOT</u> to worry about the fine.

And when Owen **RUSHES** back home, a healthy Bronco runs out to greet him.

AUTHOR

Michael Dahl is the author of more than 200 books for children and young adults. He has won the AEP Distinguished Achievement Award three times for his non-fiction. His Finnegan Zwake mystery series was shortlisted twice by the Anthony and Agatha awards. He has also written the Library of Doom series. He is a featured speaker at conferences on graphic novels and high-interest books for boys.

ILLUSTRATOR

Bradford Kendall has enjoyed drawing for as long as he can remember. As a boy, he loved to read comic books and watch old monster movies. He graduated from university with a BFA in Illustration. He has owned his own commercial art business since 1983, and lives with his wife, Leigh, and their two children, Lily and Stephen. They also have a cat named Hansel and a dog named Gretel.

GLOSSARY

brooch piece of jewellery that can be pinned to your clothes

fine sum of money paid as punishment for doing something wrong

footnote note at the bottom of a page that explains something in the text. Endnotes are the same notes, but collected at the end of a chapter or book.

injured hurt

myth story that people believe

overdue late

poisoned given a harmful substance

reference book that helps find information

scan look at quickly, to find a piece of information

signal way of sending a message

spines central, vertical pieces of book covers

Library of Doom

Sex Ht Wt Eye Color
M 1.9m 84kg Blue
THE LIBRARIAN

LIBRARIAN

Real name: unknown (may begin with a T or a G)

Parents: unknown

Birthplace/birthdate: unknown

Questions: Has he always existed? Will he ever be defeated? Are there books he doesn't protect?

Dislikes: Water, crumbs, dirty fingers

Powers: Speed reading, ability to fly, martial arts

Library of Doom

Sex · Ht · Wt · Eye Color
F · 1.7m · 68kg · Brown

THE SKYWRITER

Skywriter

Real name: Sophia (last name unknown)

Parents: unknown

Birthplace/birthdate: United Kingdom, 20th century

Questions: What is her role in protecting the Librarian? Can she be stopped?

Dislikes: Bad listeners

Powers: Ability to fly, does not need sleep, can research anything, good handwriting

INKFOOT

After leaving Ms Eel's library, the Librarian took the piece of paper containing Inkfoot's endnotes to Sywriter's lab. There, Skywriter tested the paper. Using a special kind of disappearing ink, she tried to erase the Inkfoot endnotes. It did not work.

She then tried to burn the paper. It burned, but the notes collected on a nearby notepad.

When Skywriter tried to destroy the notepad by cutting it into tiny pieces of paper, the notepad turned into a small pack of sticky notes.

They now remain in the Librarian's office, locked safely away.

Discussion Questions

1. Is it fair for a librarian to fine a student who does not **return** a book on time? Why or why not?

2. If Owen had not gone to the library, what do you think would have **HAPPENED**?

3. Owen goes to the library to work out what kind of animal could have attacked his dog. What would you have done?

WRITING PROMPTS

1. Imagine another way that the Librarian could have defeated **INKFOOT**. How does he do it? Write about it.

2. **CREATE** your own book cover. Don't forget to add the text on the back and give your book a title!

?

3. Write about your favourite book. What is it about? Who wrote it? Why is it your favourite?

?

?

More books from the Library of Doom